Henry loves yetis.
Yes, *yetis*.

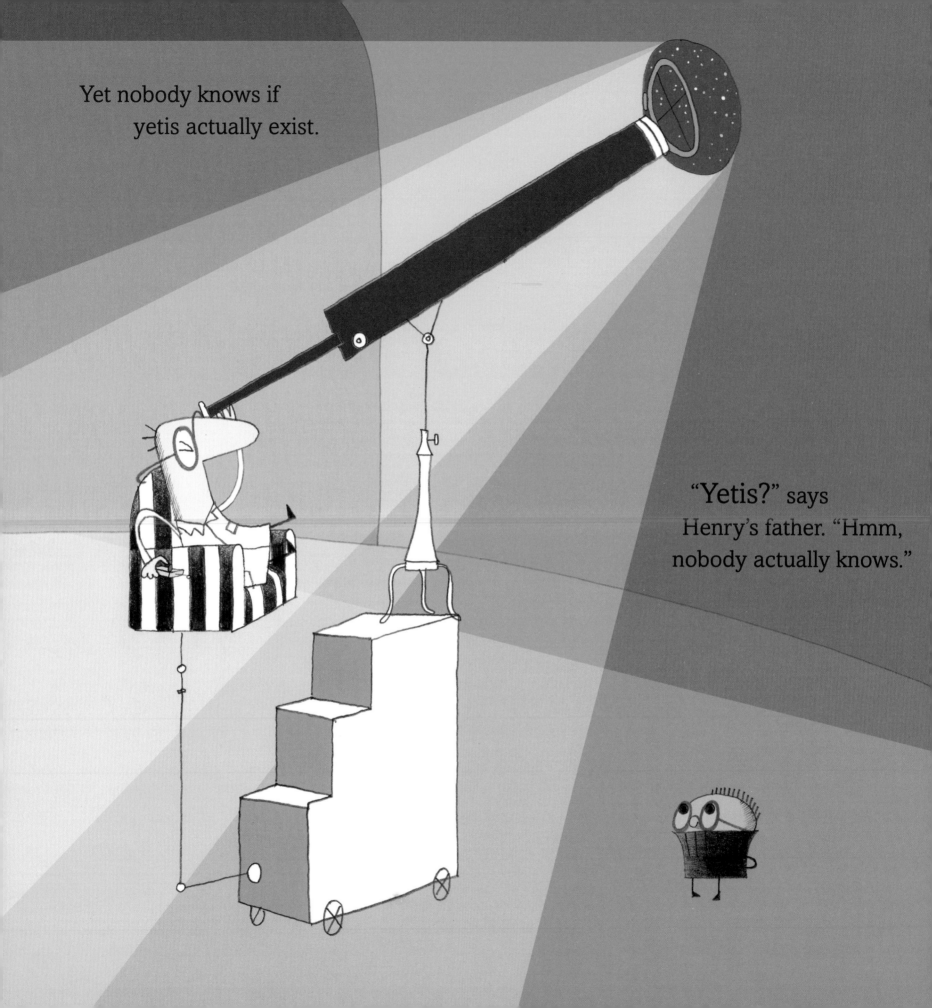

Yet nobody knows if yetis actually exist.

"Yetis?" says Henry's father. "Hmm, nobody actually knows."

But Henry is sure yetis do exist . . .

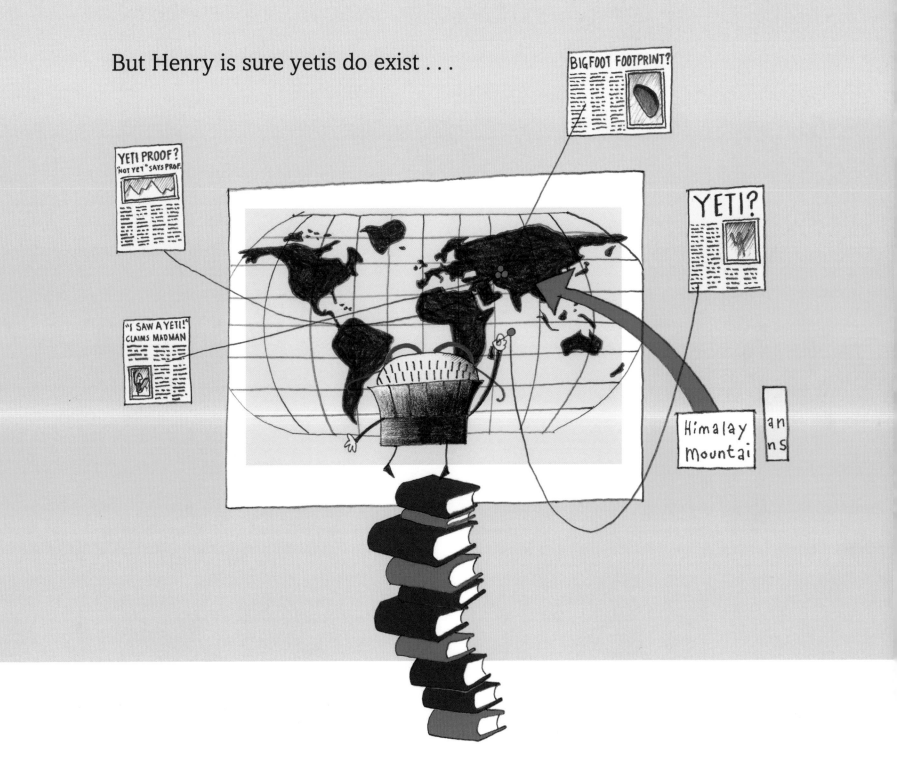

so he will go on an expedition to find one.

Henry asks his headteacher if he
can miss school to go on the expedition.

"Yetis?" says
the headteacher.
"They don't exist."

"This is a school announcement. Henry is going on an expedition to find a yeti!"

Everybody laughs.

Ha ha ha! Ha ha ha!

"And if you do happen to see one," says the headteacher, "don't forget to bring back some evidence."

Henry packs all the equipment
he needs for the expedition.

A waterproof
hammock.
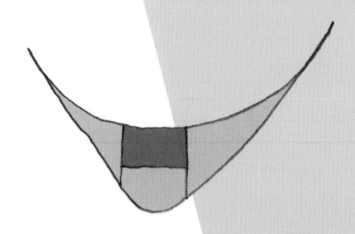

A compass.

A telescope.

A climbing rope.

And a camera to take pictures for evidence.

Now Henry is ready.

"Remember, **no** staying
up late," says Henry's father.

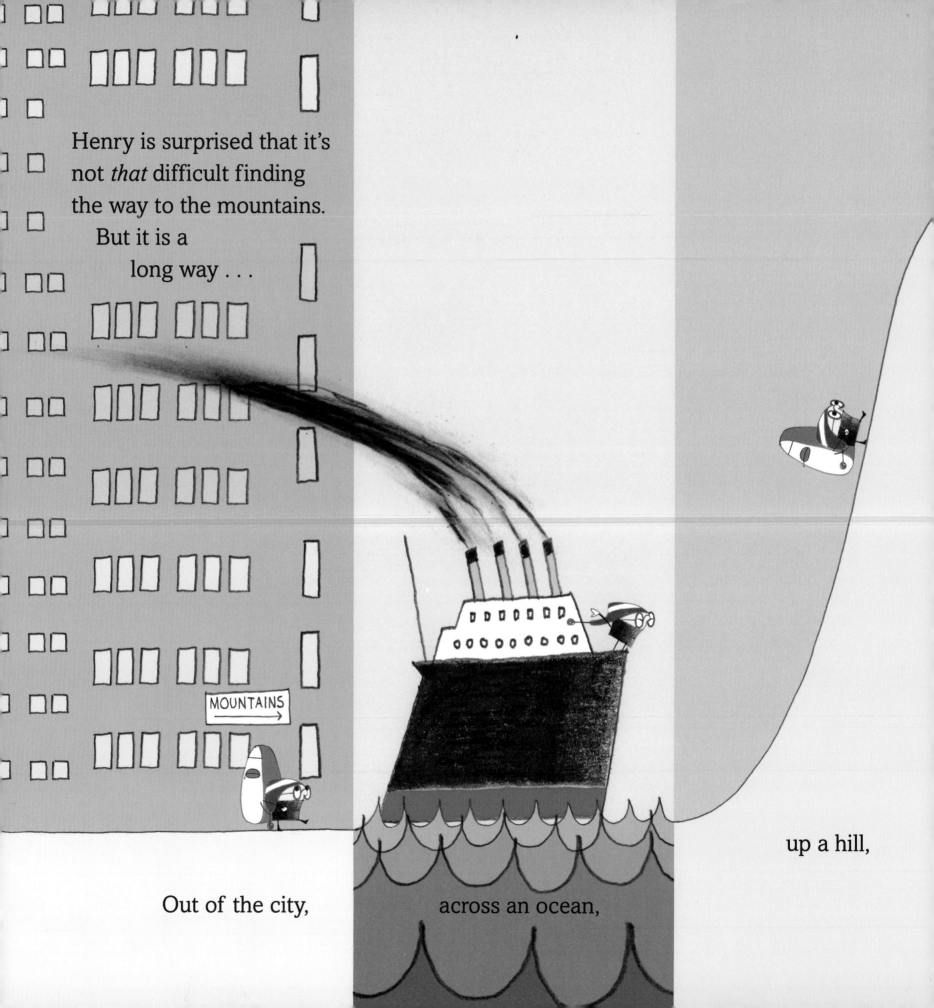

Henry is surprised that it's not *that* difficult finding the way to the mountains. But it is a long way . . .

MOUNTAINS →

Out of the city,

across an ocean,

up a hill,

over a river,

and through a dense forest
(all without staying up late),

until . . .

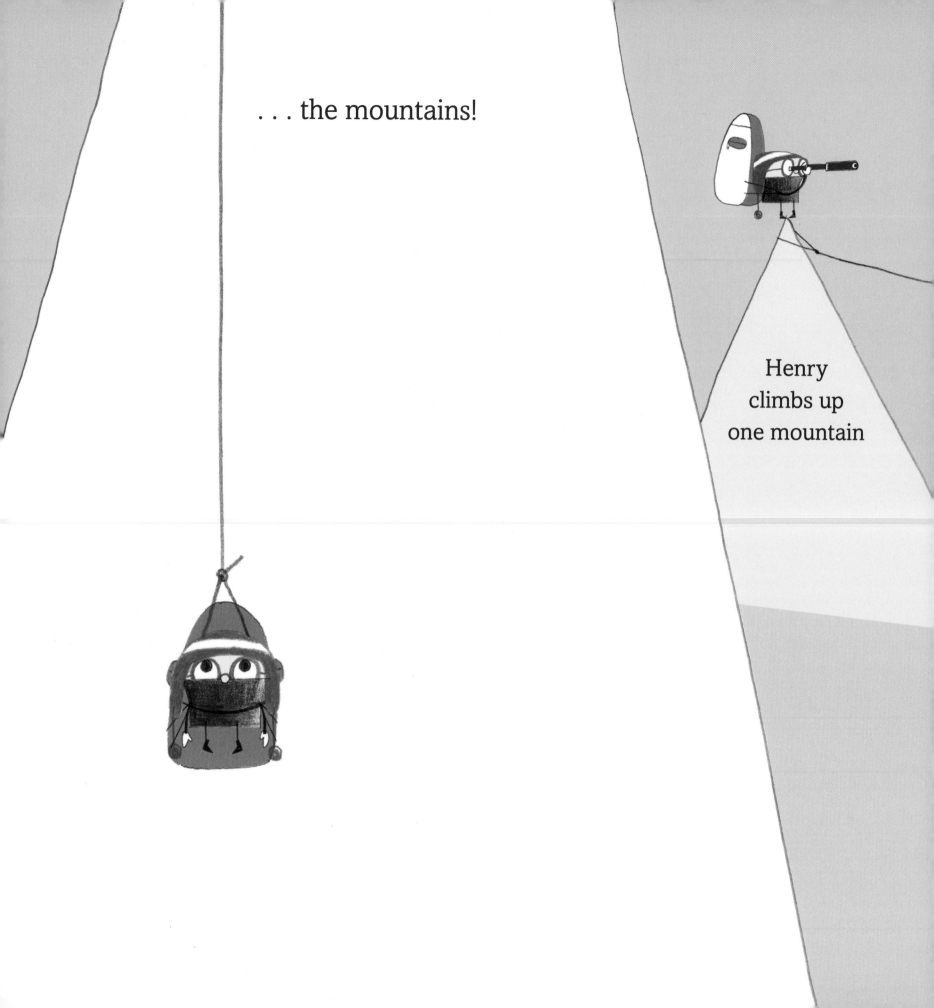

. . . the mountains!

Henry
climbs up
one mountain

after another,

searching **everywhere** for a yeti.

But Henry finds nothing.
There is no sign of a yeti anywhere.
Not even a suspicious-looking footprint.

Henry was **sure** yetis do exist,
but now he isn't so sure.

Maybe he should just turn around and go right back . . .

Oh!

Henry sees a yeti.
The yeti sees Henry.

The yeti is slightly **bigger** than Henry expects.
And more friendly.

Henry takes pictures of
the yeti for evidence.

Then they
play hide and seek.

Now it is time for Henry to go home.

Henry is surprised that it's more
difficult knowing the way back . . .

MOUNTAINS

so he uses his compass to find the right way home.

"Well?" says Henry's father.

"I didn't stay up late once," says Henry.

"No," says Henry's father. "Did you see a yeti?"

"Oh yes!" says Henry. "Yetis do exist! And I've brought back the evidence."

Henry unpacks all the equipment.

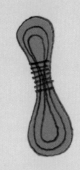

A climbing rope.

A telescope.

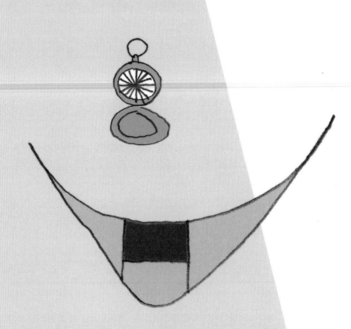

A compass.

And a waterproof
hammock.

Wait a minute!
No camera.

"No camera!"
says Henry.

"No camera, no evidence," says Henry's father.

"No evidence," says Henry.

"No evidence!" says the headteacher.

"Write me ten million lines
for making things up.
Yetis indeed!"

Everybody laughs.

Ha ha ha! Ha ha ha!

million lines! 10 million lines! 10 million line
million lines! 10 million lines! 10 million line
million lines! 10 million lines! 10 million line
million lines! 10 million lines! 10 million line
million lines! 10 million lines! 10 million line
million lines! 10 million lines! 10 million line
million lines! 10 million lines! 10 million line
million lines! 10 million lines! 10 million line
million lines! 10 million lines! 10 million line
million lines! 10 million lines! 10 million line
million lines! 10 million lines! 10 million line
million lines! 10 million lines! 10 million lin
million lines! 10 million lines! 10 million line
million lines! 10 million lines! 10 million line

What can Henry do now?
He is **not** making things up. He **did** see a yeti. Yetis **do** exist.

But nobody, except his own father, believes him.

Oh!
Henry sees the yeti again.

The yeti sees Henry.
The headteacher sees the yeti.

And everybody stops laughing.

Now the headteacher is
having a lie down.

The yeti gives Henry back his camera.

Henry is thinking he will probably **not** have to write ten million lines after all.

Henry loves yetis.
Yes, *yetis.*

THE END